# Jump
## for the
# Stars

Ash

To Theodore,
Gigi and Otto ~ V W

To my parents, thank you
for the best childhood. ~ T R-B

Cormac

Cara

Theo

Fred

Ali

First published in Great Britain 2022 by Catch a Star,
an imprint of New Frontier Publishing Europe Ltd
Vicarage House, 58-60 Kensington Church Street, London, W8 4DB
www.newfrontierpublishing.co.uk

Text © Vogue Williams 2022 • Illustrations © Tilia Rand-Bell 2022
The moral rights of the author and illustrator have been asserted.

ISBN: 978-1-915167-13-2 (HB)
ISBN: 978-1-915167-31-6 (Independent) • ISBN: 978-1-915167-32-3 (Waterstones)

A CIP record for this book is available from the British Library

Edited by Tasha Evans • Designed by Verity Clark
Printed in China

1 3 5 7 9 10 8 6 4 2

Ruby

Leo

# Vogue Williams

Quinn

# Jump

Connor

## for the Stars

Amara

Lola

Katie

Illustrated by
# Tilia Rand-Bell

CATCH a STAR

Lily

It's early in the morning,
STRETCHING is the first thing we do.

Amara's reaching for the stars,
Can you stretch with her, too?

Can you spot . . .

stars
on the
ceiling?

Ali's baby sister loves him,
He can JUGGLE balls so high.

Can you spot . . . baby's toy bunny?

Over here and over there,
They're heading for the sky!

Can you spot... a banana skin?

It's time for some breakfast,
Banana porridge is the best.

It's super YUMMY and HEALTHY,
Lily shouts, 'Be my guest!'

Can you spot . . . another friend?

Cormac and Quinn are off to nursery,
And SCOOT down the street.

They have so much fun there,
With other kids to meet.

Cara GALLOPS
Like a horse,
While Cormac
Likes to HOP.

Quinn JUMPS
Like a kangaroo,

While Ash is a cheetah,
Please Stop!!

Can you spot . . . .
a frog?

1, 2, 3,
We're coming to get Fred.
He's found a super hiding place,
Behind the flowerbed.

CATCH and IT are some of the games,
HOPSCOTCH, CLAPPING and TAG.
Where is Connor's SKIPPING rope?
It's in the teacher's bag!

Can you spot . . .

a water bottle?

a mouse?
Oh no!

Can you spot . . .

Sometimes, we have to be really quiet,
BREATHING SLOWLY, in and out.

It's time to think and rest our heads,
Katie, please don't shout.

Bees are buzzing noisily,
They're filling up the skies!

a colourful kite?

Can you spot . . .

JUMPING in and out of puddles,

Is BUCKETLOADS of fun.

If we don't stop soon,
We'll land on planet Mars!

See Lola on the dance floor,
She's giving it her MOVES.

Then Uncle clears the way again,
It's time for crazy GROOVES.

Can you spot . . .

a disco
ball?

Can you spot . . .

a pet hamster?

Leo's trying out the LION POSE,
His bottom's in the air.

His dog is joining in with him,
But Leo doesn't care.

Ruby's RELAXING in the bath,
And feeling oh so ZEN.

Can you spot . . . a pirate duck?

But her brother's splashing furiously,
She wants him to stop – but when?

A funny storybook for Theo,
While he's sitting on Daddy's knee.

He loves to LAUGH at the giraffe,
But he's oh so SLEEEPPPY!

Can you spot . . .

a clock?
Time for
bed!

# Did you
# spot everything?